FRONT STORY

ROGER STEVENS

Illustrated by Jacqui Thomas

Oxford University Press

OXFORD

UNIVERSITY PRESS

Great Clarendon Street, Oxford OX2 6DP

Oxford University Press is a department of the Unversity of Oxford.
It furthers the University's objective of excellence in research, scholarship,
and education by publishing worldwide in

Oxford New York

Auckland Bangkok Buenos Aires Cape Town Chennai
Dar es Salaam Delhi Hong Kong Istanbul Karachi Kolkata
Kuala Lumpur Madrid Melbourne Mexico City Mumbai Nairobi
São Paulo Shanghai Taipei Tokyo Toronto

Oxford is a registered trade mark of Oxford University Press
in the UK and in certain other countries

ISBN 0 19 916875 X

Printed in Great Britain

Illustrations by Jacqui Thomas c/o Linda Rogers Associates Ltd.

1

The missing money

Sam and Lisa were sitting in the reading corner trying to come up with some good ideas for stories. They'd been chosen to be reporters for the Class Six Gazette – the new class newspaper.

A journalist from their local paper had been talking to their class all morning about how newspapers were made and Mrs Moss had decided they would make their own.

The class was buzzing with excitement. Even Mrs Moss was excited and it took a lot to get her going. The last time had been when the Head walked into the pond life mobile hanging from the ceiling and got frogs tangled up in his glasses.

Sam had always thought it was stupid, anyway, having frogs in a mobile. A mobile of the Man United team – that would be more like it.

Parminder poked her head round the bookcase. 'Have you got anything you want to sell?' she asked. Parminder was collecting adverts for the Class Six Gazette. Boring, Sam thought, but the journalist had told them that advertising was important. Advertisers paid money to the paper. The money helped to pay for the paper to be printed.

'You could sell your skateboard,' Sam said to Lisa.

Lisa stuck out her tongue. 'And you could sell your Man United videos,' she said.

'You haven't got anything then,' Parminder said brightly.

Sam shook his head. 'We could try selling the school.'

'Nobody would buy it,' Parminder said, 'not if you were in it.' And she flounced off to try someone else.

Sam opened his pencil case to find
a pen. 'There must be something we can
write about. Something exciting must
have happened. What about when the
caretaker locked Mrs Moss in the school
and she set off the burglar alarm trying
to get out?'

Lisa shook her head. 'No, that was last
year. News is supposed to be up to date.'

Now Sam was digging about in his
bag. He looked puzzled.

'What's up?' Lisa asked.

'My pen. My best felt tip. It's gone.'

'That's funny,' Lisa said. 'This morning I couldn't find my bar of chocolate. I know Mum put it in my lunch box – Ouch!'

There was a crash as a pile of books landed on them. They jumped up in surprise as books flew everywhere. A grinning face poked through the gap.

'Very funny, Benny,' Sam said. 'Now clear it up.'

'Are you going to make me?' sneered Benny.

Sam went red. 'I'm not scared of you, Benny Preston – ' he started.

'Stop it, Sam,' warned Lisa. 'You know what he's like.'

Everyone was scared of Benny. And he was always picking on someone.

'That's right.' Benny grinned and pushed some more books off the shelf.

'You'll get into trouble now,' Lisa said angrily.

'Well, if I do,' Benny said, 'then my mates will have to sort you two out at playtime. So you'd better tidy up quickly.' Benny left, leaving Lisa and Sam staring glumly at the books on the floor.

Alice peeked round the corner. 'Oh dear,' she said in her rather timid voice.

'It was Benny,' Sam said.

Alice watched them tidying up the books.

'What is it?' Lisa asked her.

'Oh, I'm doing the letters page. Will you write a letter to the paper?'

Sam snorted. 'Yes. About Benny. He's a bully.'

Just then, Mrs Moss banged her coffee mug on her desk. This was how she called for quiet.

'Come here, children,' she called. 'Quickly now, it's important.'

There was a mad scramble to be either at the front or the back. Benny stood grinning and flicking bits of paper at Sally.

'I'm afraid I have some bad news,' Mrs Moss said, when the class became quiet. 'This morning I put a ten pound note in my drawer. Now it's gone. Has anyone seen it?'

There was silence.

'In that case,' she said, 'I can only think it's been stolen. I hate to say this but I think we have a thief in the class.'

2

Chasing a story

Sam and Lisa were in the playground, talking about the missing ten pounds. An icy wind chased brown leaves and empty crisp packets around and around in a mad dance.

'If we can find that ten pounds, it will make a good story,' Sam said.

Lisa nodded. 'Yes,' she said. 'That would be real news. We'd have a real story for the Class Six Gazette.'

A voice rang across the playground. 'Watchya, Big Ears.' It was Benny again.

They turned their backs on him.

'Benny!' Sam said. 'I remember now. Mrs Moss was looking at his work when she had to go to the office to get Tom's inhaler. Do you think Benny took that ten pounds? He was at her desk and she was out of the room. What do you think?'

'Maybe,' Lisa said. 'But how can we prove it?'

They thought for a moment. Benny
ran past, kicking a football. It belonged to
some kids from Class 2 and they were
yelling and screaming for their ball back.

'Listen,' Lisa said. 'If he did take the
money he'll probably spend it on the
way home. Let's follow him.'

'Brilliant,' Sam said.

The football whizzed by, just missing
Sam's head.

'Hey, Big Ears,' Benny sneered. 'Can I
have my ball back?'

Lisa and Sam were among the first out of school. It was nearly dark. They leant against the wall as the rest of the school trooped out. Cars hooted. Kids were shouting and chasing and waving at the waiting mums and dads.

At last Benny passed by with some of his mates. Sam and Lisa followed him.

It was easy at first, in the crush of children and mums and dads with pushchairs. But the crowds began thinning out as they reached the bottom of the hill where the school road met the main road through the estate.

'Where is he?' Lisa asked, peering around anxiously.

'He went in the shop,' Sam said. 'Quick, or we'll be too late. Let's see if he spends that money.'

The inside of the shop was full of children. Mr Patel, the newsagent, was getting ratty, as he always did when the kids crowded round his counter.

'One at a time, one at a time,' he kept saying, as eager hands waved money at him. Benny had already pushed to the front.

'Ten Silk Cut,' Benny said.

'You know I can't serve you cigarettes, Benny Preston,' Mr Patel said.

'They're for my mum,' Benny grinned. 'She asked me to get them on the way home.'

'No she didn't,' Mr Patel said. 'She's not that daft.'

'Well, I'll have some of those pear drops, then. Up there on the top shelf.'

Mr Patel sighed and turned to reach the big glass jar.

Sam and Lisa edged nearer. 'What's he going to do?' Lisa whispered.

Sam gripped Lisa's arm.

3

More surprises

Sam and Lisa stood in the crowded shop watching Benny. As Mr Patel grabbed the big glass jar full of pear drops Benny made a rude sign behind his back. Several children giggled.

Mr Patel put the jar on the counter. 'How many do you want?' he asked.

'None,' Benny said. 'I've changed my mind.' He turned round and pushed his way through the crowd and left the shop. Sam and Lisa followed him.

They sat on the low wall outside the
shop and watched Benny and his mates
disappear up the hill in an unruly bunch,
weaving on and off the pavement.

'So much for that,' Sam said,
disappointed. 'What now?'

Lisa shrugged. 'He didn't steal
anything. He didn't even spend that ten
pounds,' she said.

They watched as the children from their school went home – the oldest ones alone, younger ones with the mums and dads who had come to collect them. Soon Sam and Lisa were alone.

'Perhaps he's not the thief,' Lisa said.

'But I'm sure it's him,' Sam said. 'We'll just have to keep an eye on him in class tomorrow.'

'Listen,' Lisa said. 'If we find that ten pounds it can be the front page story in the Gazette.'

'Yes,' Sam said, brightening up. 'Thief unmasked by Sam Scoop, ace reporter.'

'And Lisa Jones,' Lisa reminded him. 'But there's one big problem.'

'What's that?'

'We have to find the thief first.'

'Oh yes,' Sam said glumly.

'Look, here comes Alice.' Lisa pointed.

Alice walked slowly towards them, trailing her school bag. Her eyes were red. It looked as if she'd been crying.

'What's up?' Lisa asked.

'Mum didn't meet me from school,'
Alice said. 'She promised she would today.'

'I expect she forgot,' Sam said. 'My mum
forgot me once. I waited all night. Next
morning I was the first at school.'

'Don't lie,' Lisa said. 'It's okay, Alice,' she
went on. 'He's just being stupid. We'll walk
with you if you like.'

'Yes,' Sam said. 'There's no need to cry.'

Alice started sobbing. 'It's not just Mum
not turning up, it's something else.'

'What?' Lisa asked.

Alice thought for a moment, then shook her head. 'Nothing,' she said. 'I'll be okay.' Sam and Lisa watched her go.

'I wonder what all that was about,' Lisa said. 'She seemed very upset.'

'Another mystery,' Sam added.

'Well, I've had enough mysteries for today and now I want my tea. I'm going home,' Lisa said. 'I'll see you tomorrow.'

Sam nodded. 'And we'll keep our eyes open. We could set a trap.'

Lisa stared. 'What do you mean?' she said.

'We could catch the thief ourselves,' Sam explained.

'Just us two? Don't be daft,' Lisa said.

'But I've got an idea,' insisted Sam. 'I'll tell you tomorrow.'

'Well, I'm off home. See you.'

'Bye.' Sam watched her go. Yes, he decided. That's what they'd do tomorrow. They'd set a trap for the thief.

4

The trap

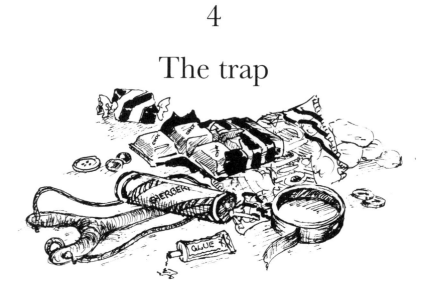

The class was silent. Mrs Moss stood at the front. Her voice was stern.

'And so, unless I find the ten pounds today there will be no playtime. You'll all stay in and work instead. And there will be no class newspaper.'

There was a groan and everyone started talking at once.

'Quiet!' Mrs Moss shouted. 'That sort of noise isn't going to help, is it? Now – get out your reading books. You'll read silently for the next twenty minutes.'

Benny put his hand up. 'I've finished my book,' he said.

'Then read it again,' Mrs Moss thundered. Benny nudged the boy sitting next to him and grinned.

'Total silence,' Mrs Moss said. 'I mean it.'

At lunch time Sam and Lisa sat together in the hall where everyone ate their packed lunches.

'I've never seen Mrs Moss so mad,' Sam said.

'Me neither.'

Sam opened his lunch box. 'What have you got?' Lisa asked him.

'Jam and peanut butter.'

Lisa pulled a face.

They ate in silence. 'Do you think your plan will work?' Lisa said at last.

'Of course it will,' Sam said. 'Look.' He took his Gameboy out of his pocket.

'Put it away quickly, before the dinner ladies see it,' Lisa said. 'You're not allowed those in school.'

Sam quickly slipped it back in his pocket. 'All the class know I've got my Gameboy at school. Now, this is the plan. The classroom will be empty this dinner time, right?'

Lisa nodded.

'We'll go there now and leave the Gameboy on my desk. If someone wants to steal things, they'll try this dinner time when there's nobody about.'

Sam went on, 'All we have to do is keep watch. If one of our class goes into the school we follow them. Whoever it is will see the Gameboy on my table. They're bound to take it. Then, we go into the classroom and catch the thief red handed. What do you think?'

'I don't know,' Lisa said. 'Isn't it … well, won't we be encouraging someone to steal? It doesn't seem right, somehow. And how will we prove the Gameboy is yours? Loads of people have got Gameboys.'

'I used my dad's security pen to put my name on it,' Sam said.

'But won't you get into trouble for bringing it to school in the first place?' said Lisa.

Sam shrugged. 'Mrs Moss will only tell me off and lock it up till we go home.'

'But what if it *is* Benny,' Lisa said.

'What do you mean?'

'Well, he might not give us the Gameboy back.'

'We'll take some others with us. He'll back down if his mates aren't there. He always does.'

'But what do we do then?' said Lisa.

'We'll say we know he takes things now. If he takes anything else, we'll tell Mrs Moss. He'll know he can't get away with it any longer. He'll own up about the ten pounds.'

'Do you really think the plan will work?' Lisa asked.

'Of course it will. Trust me.' Sam took a big bite of his sandwich.

He stopped chomping as Lisa groaned, 'Oh no.'

'What?' Sam asked, showering bits of bread everywhere.

'My bar of chocolate. It's gone again.'

Sam and Lisa were in the school field watching a game of football. Sam was feeling worried. It was nearly time for afternoon school and nothing had happened. Sam was scared that Mrs Moss would go back to the classroom and find the Gameboy first. Then he'd be the one to get into trouble.

Suddenly Parminder came running up, out of breath. 'Quick,' she panted. 'It's Benny. He's just gone into the school.'

5

Who is the thief?

Parminder, Sam and Lisa, Sally and Tom stood in a huddle outside the classroom. The plan seemed to be working. Benny was in the classroom. Now they would find out if he really was the thief.

'Let's go in,' Sam whispered. 'He must have found the Gameboy by now.'

'Wait a bit longer,' Lisa whispered back. 'We've got to give Benny plenty of time.' Sam looked around anxiously. 'But a dinner lady will come along any minute. Or a teacher. Then what will we do?'

They waited a bit longer. The tension was unbearable. There was a knot in Sam's stomach.

'Now?' Sam whispered.

'Okay,' Lisa said.

They all trooped into the classroom. Sam looked quickly around. The Gameboy was no longer on his table.

There was Benny. 'Hi, Big Ears,' he sneered. 'Have you come in to do some extra work?'

'Where's my Gameboy?' Sam asked.

'I don't know what you mean,' Benny replied.

'We think you've stolen it,' Lisa said.

Benny laughed. 'Prove it. What are you going to do? Search me?'

Sam swallowed. He felt nervous. 'Yes, if we have to,' he said.

Benny's grin turned to a scowl. 'Just try it!'

By now the others were crowding around him. Tom spoke. 'Are you going to hit us all, then?' he asked.

Benny raised his fists as though he was about to fight. Sam held his breath. But Benny seemed less sure of himself now. He looked at everyone crowding round him. Then he looked past them, at the classroom door, hoping that his mates would come and help him out. Then he put his hands down and shrugged.

He pulled the Gameboy from his pocket and tossed it on to the table where it fell with a clatter. 'It's a load of rubbish anyway,' he said.

'You're the class thief,' Sam told him.

'You can't prove it,' Benny smirked.

'Listen,' Lisa said. 'You've been caught red handed. If anything else goes missing we'll know it was you and we'll tell Mrs Moss. We'll tell her the whole story.'

Benny fidgeted and said nothing.

'Okay?' Sam asked, feeling braver now.

Benny realized they had won. 'Okay,' he muttered.

'Now where's the ten pounds?' Lisa asked him.

Benny looked up in surprise. 'I don't know. I didn't steal it.'

'Yes you did,' Sam accused him.

'I didn't,' Benny protested. 'I'm not that stupid.'

Suddenly Benny pushed past them and ran to the door.

'I didn't take the money,' he cried. 'You can say what you like but I didn't take it.' Then he was gone, slamming the door behind him.

Sam picked up the Gameboy and looked to see if it was broken. It wasn't.

'You know what?' Lisa said quietly.

'What?' Sam asked.

'I believe him. I don't think Benny did take the money.'

'Then who did?' Sam asked.

6

Gazette makes the news

'Close your books,' Mrs Moss said. 'I've got something important to tell you.'

The afternoon's lessons had begun with silent reading. Mrs Moss had called the register in a quiet voice. Usually, calling the register was fun and Mrs Moss made jokes as she called out the names. But not today.

'The money still hasn't been found,' Mrs Moss said.

A murmur went round the class. Sam caught Benny's eye. Benny stared back at him defiantly.

Mrs Moss went on, 'I've talked with the head teacher and we've decided that we are going to send a letter home to your parents. Maybe they can help us find the ten pounds.'

Suddenly Alice burst into tears. She got up from her table and rushed out of the classroom.

'Carry on reading in silence until I get back,' Mrs Moss ordered sternly.

As soon as she had gone, everyone started talking.

'Well, what do you make of that?' Lisa asked Sam.

He shook his head. 'I don't know. But I guess we'll soon find out.'

Mrs Moss came back. 'I think we've found our ten pounds,' she said gently. There was total silence in the classroom. You could have heard a stick of chalk drop.

Alice must have known who the thief was all along. Perhaps it was Benny after all, Sam thought. Perhaps Benny had made Alice promise not to say anything.

Who was the thief? Everyone watched
Mrs Moss. But Mrs Moss did not look
angry. Instead she looked sad. 'It
was Alice,' she said.

Several of the class gasped in surprise.
The silence hung in the air for several
seconds. Alice? She wouldn't steal
money. There must be some mistake.
Then everyone started talking at once.

'Quiet!' said Mrs Moss. 'Now listen. The head has taken Alice home to talk to her mum. It was very, very wrong of Alice to steal the money and she will have to be punished, but she had a reason. Her little brother, Daniel, is very ill. He may even die.' Mrs Moss stopped speaking for a moment. She looked sad.

'But there is a chance of saving him,' she went on, 'He has a rare form of cancer and there is a way it can be cured. But he needs an operation that can only be done in America. Alice thought that the ten pounds she stole would help to pay for it.'

Parminder put her hand up.

'Yes, Parminder?'

'But it costs hundreds of pounds to fly to America,' Parminder said.

'And probably thousands for the operation,' Sally added.

'That's right,' their teacher went on. 'Alice isn't really a bad girl but she's very upset at the moment. As I said, she will have to be punished.'

Mrs Moss looked hard at the class. 'But when she comes back tomorrow I want you all to be kind to her. Think what she must have gone through. And please – don't talk about this to anyone else. The poor girl has enough problems as it is.'

Sam put his hand up.

'Yes, Sam?'

'Are we going to carry on with the newspaper, then?'

'Yes you are,' Mrs Moss said.

The class cheered.

Lisa put up her hand. 'Couldn't we write about Alice's brother in the Class Six Gazette? We could raise money for him, like they do in real newspapers.'

Mrs Moss thought for a moment. 'Start a campaign, you mean?'

Lisa nodded. 'Yes, a campaign. We could try to raise the money for Daniel's fare.'

'Brilliant!' Sam added. 'And we might get the local paper to help. Can we phone the reporter who came to talk to us?'

'Well, I'll have to talk to the head about it first,' Mrs Moss said, smiling, 'but it sounds like a good idea to me and I'm sure the head will agree.'

Sam and Lisa wrote their story for the Class Six Gazette. It had a big headline which said HELP CLASS SIX TO SAVE LITTLE DAN. Everyone in the class began to collect money. Even Benny Preston joined in. Soon, all the children at the school and their mums and dads wanted to help.

By the end of the next day they had £200 in the campaign fund, and lots of people to help them collect more.

Sam and Lisa phoned the local paper from the school office. Lisa talked to the reporter, who was very interested. She promised to go to see Alice's mum and to visit the school again.

'What else did she say?' Sam asked eagerly.

'Well, she said she can't promise anything but she thinks it is a good story. She thinks they can probably raise enough money for the operation and the air fares. She said that the Class Six Gazette will get into the paper, too.'

'Great,' Sam said, smiling. 'That's brilliant. Sam Scoop in Class Six Gazette Mercy Mission – I mean –'

'Sam Scoop *and* Lisa Jones,' finished Lisa, and they both laughed.

About the author

I was a teacher in a Primary
School but I really wanted
to write. It took a lot of
stories and poems before
my first book was
published.

I live in Nottingham
with my wife who was
once a newspaper editor.
Between us we have three children,
Paul, Kate, and Joseph. I also play in a band
and visit schools to read and talk about my
poems and stories.

When I first told this story, a teacher called
Mrs Moss thought I must have made it up about
her. I hadn't. But that goes to show that stories
can be just like real life.

Other books at Stages 12, 13, and 14 include:

Billy's Luck by Paul Shipton
Cool Clive by Michaela Morgan
Call 999! by Sylvia Moody
Pet Squad by Paul Shipton
Sing for your Supper by Nick Warburton

Also available in packs
Stages 12/13/14 pack A   0 19 916879 2
Stages 12/13/14 class pack A   0 19 916880 6